# A FLYING DAY

10  9  8  7  6  5  4  3  2  1

British Library Cataloguing in Publication Data available.

ISBN 0 86264 337 6

This book has been printed on acid-free paper

# ANN TURNBULL
# A FLYING DAY
## Illustrated by KEN BROWN

Andersen Press · London

"It's a drying day," said the woman.
She washed her net curtains, and a tablecloth, and a
shirt. She hung them on the line to dry.

The wind caught the washing line and swung it to and fro. The tablecloth slapped and cracked. The net curtains flung out spray. The sleeves of the shirt filled up with air.

"It's a drying day," said the net curtains. They billowed in the wind.

"It's a drying day," said the tablecloth. It flapped like a flag as the line lifted.

The shirt jerked and jumped and punched the air with wind-fat sleeves.

"It's a flying day!" it said. "Let me go, pegs. I want to fly."

The wind blew harder. It blew so hard that the net curtains and the tablecloth wound themselves round and round and round the line. It blew so hard that the pegs holding the shirt flew off – pop! pop! – into the bushes.

The shirt was free.

"It's a flying day!" sang the shirt. It flew up, high, higher into the air. It flew over the bushes and into next-door's garden.

Next door's cat was sunbathing on the wall. He swiped at the shirt as it flew overhead.

"Where are you off to?" he said.

"Who knows?" said the shirt. "Fresh air, freedom, adventure."

"Shirts don't have adventures," retorted the cat. He disliked the way the wind was ruffling his fur. "Someone should be wearing you."

"Someone does," said the shirt. "He wears me in a hot office. He tightens my throat with a tie. He wears me in his hot car. He never takes me out in the fresh air. But I've escaped!"

And the wind seized the shirt and blew it up like a balloon, sweeping it high, higher over the tree tops.

A flock of pigeons went by. They circled the chimney pots, turning all together with a flash of white.

"It's a flying day!" they called.

"I'll fly with you!" said the shirt.

But the pigeons sped away, and when the wind dropped, the shirt dropped with it and was snagged on a thorn hedge. The thorns caught fast.

"Help me, wind!" cried the shirt.

The wind blew. The shirt fought the thorns. The wind blew harder. The shirt struggled and tugged, and the thorns were ripped away as it pulled itself free.

Ragged, but triumphant, it sailed up into the sky.
It was blown over a playing field. Far below was a game
of football; people were running to and fro. The shirt
was blown higher. Seagulls flew around it.

"It's a flying day!" said the seagulls. "We follow the
rivers. We sail on the wind."

"I'll sail with you!" said the shirt.

But it had no wings. And when the wind dropped, the shirt dropped with it, down into the muddy football field. It blew against a player's legs and he tripped and fell and the shirt was crushed and covered in mud.

"Seagulls, wait!" called the shirt.

But the seagulls had all flown away.

Someone picked up the shirt and tossed it off the pitch.
Two boys grabbed it.
They said, "Look! A dirty old shirt!" and chased each
other with it. When they tired of their game they threw
the shirt over a hedge.

It fell onto a path and lay there – torn, muddy, and too wet to fly.

"My flying days are over," said the shirt.

Nearby it heard birds scolding. The path where the shirt lay was next to the allotments. Seedlings were growing there.

The birds were angry because the man who owned the nearest allotment was making a scarecrow. The man made the body with sticks and he stuffed a sack with rags to make a head. He stood back and looked at his scarecrow.

"I need some old clothes," he decided, "something that will flap."

He saw the shirt lying on the path. He picked it up and shook it out.

"Here's just the thing!" he said.

The man put the shirt on the scarecrow. The wind blew and the shirt-tails flapped and snapped. The wind filled the shirt like a sail. The sleeves grew fat; they punched the air. Blackbirds and sparrows flew away in fright.

"This is the life for me!" said the shirt. "No more ties; no more offices; no more cars. I shall live out here in the fresh air forever. And every day will be a flying day."